DATE DUE

FOLLETT

Little Sister

Karen's Pizza Party
Ann M. Martin

Illustrations by Susan Tang

A
LITTLE APPLE
PAPERBACK

SCHOLASTIC INC.
New York Toronto London Auckland Sydney

No part of this publication may be reproduced in whole or in part, or stored in a retrieval system, or transmitted in any form or by any means, electronic, mechanical, photocopying, recording, or otherwise, without written permission of the publisher. For information regarding permission, write to Scholastic Inc., 730 Broadway, New York, NY 10003.

ISBN 0-590-47042-6

12 11 10 9 8   9/90123/0

Printed in the U.S.A.   40

First Scholastic printing, October 1993

*This book is for
Morgan and Katie,
Heather, Liz, Melissa, Kelly,
Angie, Claudia, Andrea L., Andrea R.,
Alison, Lindsay, and Jennifer!*

Hootie

"Do you know what Sari did yesterday?" asked my best friend Hannie Papadakis. "She used my mom's lipsticks to fill in four pages in her coloring book. The lipsticks are ruined."

"Little sisters and brothers are pests," I said.

"Not Danny," said Nancy Dawes. (She is my other best friend.)

"That's because Danny is just a baby," I replied. "Wait until he gets older. You'll see."

"Well, little brothers and sisters are not *always* pests," said Hannie.

"No, but Bobby Gianelli is," I said, and we giggled.

Hannie and Nancy and I were sitting on some desks in the back of our classroom one morning. We are in second grade at Stoneybrook Academy. Ms. Colman is our teacher. I am very lucky. I am lucky because my best friends and I are in the same class. And I am lucky because Ms. Colman is a gigundoly wonderful teacher. I just love her. The only unlucky thing is Bobby Gianelli. He is in our class, too. And he is not just a pest. He is a bully.

I am Karen Brewer. I am seven years old. I wear glasses. I have blonde hair and blue eyes and some freckles. And I love school as much as I love Ms. Colman — even if I do not love Bobby. Here are some good things about my class: We have a pet guinea pig. His name is Hootie. My husband is in the class. His name is Ricky Torres. (Of course, he is just my pretend husband. We got married on the playground one day.)

"Good morning, boys and girls," said Ms. Colman when she came into the classroom that day. "Please take your seats."

I hopped off the desk. " 'Bye," I said sadly to Hannie and Nancy. They get to sit together in the back of the room, but I have to sit in the front row. That is because I wear glasses. Ms. Colman made up the rule. She wears glasses herself. Oh well. At least I get to sit next to Ricky, since he is another glasses-wearer.

"Class," began Ms. Colman, "I have an announcement to make." (Goody! I thought. My teacher is always making Surprising Announcements.) "As you know, quite a bit of work was done on our school over the summer, especially in the cafeteria and the auditorium. Unfortunately, the work was not finished. The classrooms were supposed to have been painted. And they needed a few repairs. Yesterday the teachers had a meeting. We decided not to wait until next summer to finish the work.

We would rather see it finished now. So one by one, each of the classrooms will close for about a week to be painted and fixed up. While our room is closed, we will work in the cafeteria, the auditorium, or any empty space. We will move around a lot. That will be fine for us, but it will not be fine for Hootie. We cannot move him around all day. So we need to find a home for our guinea pig that week."

"I will take him!" I called out. (I forgot to raise my hand.)

"Thank you, Karen," said Ms. Colman. "That is a nice offer. But you need permission. So tonight, girls and boys, please tell your parents about Hootie. If any of you is interested in taking care of him for a week, bring in a note from your parents."

Well, I would certainly remember to do that. I love animals. I have two cats, two dogs, two goldfish, and my very own rat. They do not all live in one house, though. That is because I do not live in one house. I live in two houses. I am a two-two.

A Home for Hootie

What is a two-two? A two-two is someone like me, who has two families. I did not always have two families, though. A long time ago, when I was very little, I had just one — Mommy, Daddy, Andrew, and me. (Andrew is my brother. He is four now, going on five.) We lived in a big house here in Stoneybrook, Connecticut. I thought we were happy, but I guess we were not. Mommy and Daddy began to fight. Not just a little. They fought a lot. Finally, they said they were going to get a divorce, because

5

they did not love each other anymore. (They still loved Andrew and me very much, though.) After the divorce, Mommy moved to a little house, and Daddy stayed in the big house. (He grew up in that house.)

Guess what happened then. Mommy and Daddy each got married again. Mommy married a man named Seth Engle. He is my stepfather. Daddy married a woman named Elizabeth Thomas. She is my stepmother. And that is how Andrew and I got two families, one at Mommy's little house, one at Daddy's big house. Mostly we live at the little house. But every other weekend, and on some holidays and vacations, we live at the big house.

This is my little-house family: Mommy, Seth, Andrew, me, Midgie, Rocky, and Emily Junior. Midgie and Rocky are Seth's dog and cat. Emily Junior is my rat.

This is my big-house family: Daddy, Elizabeth, Kristy, Sam, Charlie, David Michael, Emily Michelle, Nannie, Andrew, me,

Shannon, Boo-Boo, Goldfishie, and Crystal Light the Second. Kristy, Sam, Charlie, and David Michael are Elizabeth's kids (Elizabeth was married once before she met Daddy), so they are my stepsister and stepbrothers. Kristy is thirteen and she babysits a lot. I just love having a big sister. Sam and Charlie go to high school. David Michael is seven like me, but he does not go to my school.

Emily Michelle is my adopted sister. She is two and a half. Daddy and Elizabeth adopted her from the faraway country of Vietnam. Sometimes Emily is a pest, but mostly she is okay. (I named my rat after her.)

Nannie is Elizabeth's mother. That makes her my stepgrandmother. Nannie helps take care of the house and all us kids.

Shannon, Boo-Boo, Goldfishie, and Crystal Light are the big-house pets. Shannon is David Michael's puppy. Boo-Boo is a fat old cat. Guess what Goldfishie and Crystal Light are. (Andrew named Goldfishie.)

Now do you understand why Andrew and I are two-twos? We have two houses and two families, two mommies and two daddies, two cats and two dogs. We have toys and clothes and books at the little house, and other toys and clothes and books at the big house. Plus I have my two best friends. Hannie lives across the street from Daddy, and Nancy lives next door to Mommy. I even have two pairs of glasses. The blue pair is for reading, the pink pair is for the rest of the time.

Mostly, I like being a two-two. But sometimes it can be confusing. For instance, if I wanted to take care of Hootie, which house would he go to? Probably the little house, but I could not be sure.

"Mommy?" I said when I came home from school that day. "Pretty soon Hootie will need a home for a week. Can we take him? Please? All you have to do is write a note to Ms. Colman."

Mommy and I talked about caring for Hootie. "Will you be responsible for him,

Karen?" asked Mommy. "Taking care of Hootie might be a big job. I do not want any trouble."

"I will be very responsible," I replied. "I promise."

"Okay," said Mommy. "Then I will talk to Daddy."

Pizza Express

That night Mommy called Daddy. They talked about Hootie, in case Hootie had to spend any time at the big house. Daddy said Hootie was welcome, so Mommy wrote a note to Ms. Colman.

The next morning I ran into my classroom. I was waving the note around over my head. "Hootie can come to my house! Hootie can come to my house!" I cried. "Look, everybody!"

"Hey, just a minute!" said Hank Reubens. (Hank is one of Ricky's good friends.)

"Hootie is going to come home with *me*. I have a note from *my* parents."

"No, Hootie is going to come home with *me*," called another voice. Addie Sidney scooted into the room in her wheelchair. "I have a note, too."

"Well, so do I," said Leslie Morris.

"So do we," said Terri and Tammy, the twins.

Uh-oh.

My classmates and I waited for Ms. Colman to arrive. When she did, we pounced on her with the notes.

"*Everybody* wants to take Hootie home," I said. "And we all have permission."

"Maybe we could take turns with Hootie," suggested Hank. "We could each take him home for one day."

"No," said Ms. Colman. "I do not think Hootie would want to be moved around so much. Let me think about what to do. I will make a decision in a few days. Okay, now. Time to get to work."

* * *

When school was over that day, Hannie and Nancy and I ran outside together. Hannie's mother was going to take us shopping. She was waiting for us with Sari and Linny. (Sari is Hannie's little sister, the one who ruined the lipsticks. Linny is Hannie's older brother.)

Mrs. Papadakis drove downtown. We hopped out of the car. Linny cried, "Toy store first!"

But we did not go to the toy store first. That was because we passed Pizza Express on the way. Pizza Express is a restaurant that sells very delicious pizza. And in the window was a sign that said CONTEST INSIDE! YOU COULD BE THE NEXT PIZZA KING OR PIZZA QUEEN! ENTER NOW! Next to the sign was a big photo of a boy wearing a gold crown.

"A contest!" I exclaimed. "Hey, let's go in! Please, Mrs. Papadakis? I would like to be the next Pizza Queen."

"Me too!" said Nancy and Hannie.

So we all went inside. "Excuse me," I

said to the woman behind the cash register. "What is a Pizza Queen? What does she do?"

"She gets to be queen for a month," said the woman. "She is in the ads for Pizza Express. Her face will appear on the billboard outside of town, and she will even be in a TV commercial. She might make some appearances in the restaurant, too. Oh, and she will receive a prize of a thousand dollars. You should enter the contest. The winner's name will be drawn next week. Then this month's Pizza King will hand over his crown to the winner. You can enter as many times as you want," she added.

My mouth dropped open. I stared at my friends. This was too good to be true. Queen for a month? My face on a billboard and in a TV commercial? A thousand dollars?

"Come on, let's enter!" I cried.

Mrs. Papadakis and Sari waited while Nancy, Hannie, Linny, and I filled out form after form. We all wanted to win.

"Come back next Thursday afternoon for the drawing!" called the woman behind the cash register as we were leaving. "Good luck!"

I decided I would keep my fingers crossed until Thursday.

Karen's Lucky Day

I did not really keep my fingers crossed for a week. I tried, but it was too hard to eat. So I just crossed my fingers whenever I thought of it.

On Thursday morning I hopped out of bed. It was Pizza Queen day. Something else happened on Thursday, though.

Ms. Colman made a Surprising Announcement.

"Boys and girls," she said, "I have decided what to do about Hootie. I have put all the notes from your parents in this shoebox." (Ms. Colman pointed to a box on her desk.) "I am going to mix them up, close my eyes, and choose one. The winner will take care of Hootie while our room is being painted. Does that seem fair?"

"Yes!" said my classmates.

Ms. Colman shuffled the papers around. She squeezed her eyes shut. Then she reached into the box and pulled out a piece of paper. She opened her eyes. "And the note is from . . ." she said slowly, "Karen's mother! Karen Brewer will take care of Hootie for us."

Karen Brewer. That was me! I had been so busy thinking about Pizza Express that I had hardly been listening to Ms. Colman. But she had said my name. I had won!

"Yea!" I cried. "Thank you, Ms. Colman."

"Hootie will go home with you in three weeks," my teacher told me. "Three weeks from tomorrow, on a Friday. You will take care of him for the weekend, the next week, and the weekend after that. Then Hootie can return to our classroom."

I nodded solemnly. I had been given an important job.

"Mommy, guess what!" I exclaimed. "Hootie is going to come home with *me*! Ms. Colman put all the notes in a box, and she chose yours!"

It was Thursday afternoon. School was over. Mommy was driving Andrew and me to Pizza Express. I could not wait to see who would be the next Pizza King or Pizza Queen.

"Karen, that is wonderful news," said Mommy. "I know you will take good care of Hootie. You are very responsible with pets."

"Thank you," I replied.

Mommy parked the car downtown. We could already see a crowd of people at Pizza Express. There were Hannie and Linny and Nancy and Ricky and Bobby and some other kids in my class. There were their parents. There were a bunch of people I did not know. Also there were some people carrying fancy cameras.

"Look!" I cried.

"I think those people are from the newspaper," said Mommy. "I guess they are going to take pictures of the winner. This is quite a contest."

"Hey, who's that?" asked Andrew. He was pointing to a boy in the window of Pizza Express. The boy was sitting on a throne and wearing a beautiful gold crown. He was smiling at the crowd.

"That must be the old Pizza King," I told Andrew. "And try to remember not to point. It isn't polite."

Andrew looked as if he were going to say something, but he did not have a chance. Just then a man waved to the crowd. He was standing in the doorway to Pizza Express, and he was holding a microphone. "Good afternoon," he said. "Welcome to the Pizza Express Royalty Contest. Today we will choose a new Pizza King or Queen.

And we will say good-bye to Rodney Harris, the reigning king. Now without further ado . . ." The man reached into a huge barrel. It was full of the entry forms we had filled out. He chose one form. "And the winner is," he said, "Karen Brewer!"

The Pizza Queen

I turned to Mommy. "Did he say my name?" I whispered.

Mommy grinned at me. "Yes!"

Suddenly I realized everyone was calling to me. Hannie and Nancy pushed through the crowd. They began jumping up and down. "Karen! You are the Pizza Queen!" exclaimed Nancy.

Ricky found me, too. "I cannot believe it! My wife is the queen! I wonder if that makes me the king."

"Karen? Karen Brewer? Where is she?" I heard someone say.

Then the man with the microphone called my name again. "Is Karen Brewer here?" he asked. "Will she please step forward?"

"Come with me, Mommy," I said.

Mommy and Andrew and I squeezed through the crowd. "Here she is," Mommy said to the man.

The man leaned toward me. "Congratulations, Karen. You are the new Pizza Express Pizza Queen. Will you please come with me?"

Click, click. "Smile, Karen!" The photographers were taking pictures.

The man led me inside Pizza Express. "I am Mr. Rush," he said on the way. "I am the owner of Pizza Express. Now if you will just join Rodney here in the window, I will crown you."

Mr. Rush helped me into the window. I looked outside. I could see Mommy and Andrew and my friends and the rest of the crowd. They were waving to me. I waved back. I did not feel so nervous.

Next to me was Rodney the Pizza King. He was still wearing the crown. But he was no longer sitting on his throne.

Mr. Rush lifted the crown from Rodney's head. "Thank you, Rodney. You have been a wonderful king," he said. Then he set the crown on my head. "Queen Karen," he went on, "long may you reign. Please be seated on your throne."

I sat on the throne. On my head was the gold crown. I really did feel like a queen. I felt lucky, too. First Hootie, then the Pizza Queen. Today was my lucky, lucky day.

After awhile the crowd drifted away. Mommy and Andrew came inside with Mr. Rush. They helped me out of the window. (I hated to leave my throne, but at least I was still wearing the crown.) We went into Mr. Rush's office.

"Let me tell you about Karen's duties," he said to Mommy. "She will be in all of the Pizza Express ads for the next month. Actually, for a bit more than a month. As

soon as possible, we will set up a photo shoot for her. We will use her pictures on posters and on the billboard outside of town. Also, she will star in a TV commercial that will be shown on the local cable channels. And we will ask her to make several appearances as the Pizza Queen. For her work, she will be paid one thousand dollars. How does that sound to you?"

Mommy looked at me. "Karen? Do you think you can handle this? It will be a big job."

"I can handle it," I replied.

So Mr. Rush asked Mommy to sign a piece of paper. Then he wrote out a check. He handed it to Mommy.

"Thank you," said Mommy. She looked a little dazed.

"My pleasure," said Mr. Rush. "Okay. Karen's first duty will be filming the TV commercial. We will need her on Saturday. I will give you the details tomorrow. I look forward to working with you."

On the way home in the car I wore my

crown. "Mommy?" I said. "May I have the check?"

Mommy shook her head. "Sorry, honey. It goes into your college fund."

I did not care. As long as I could wear the crown.

The TV Star

"The Pizza Queen, the Pizza Queen, I am the Pizza Queen." I hummed softly to myself as I got dressed. It was Saturday morning on a big-house weekend. Later in the day I would make my debut as a commercial actress. The TV people had said it did not matter what I wore to the studio. They would give me an outfit there. So I put on blue jeans, a striped T-shirt, and my shoes that look like ballet slippers. Then I put on my crown. I had been wearing the crown since Thursday (except when I was asleep).

I had even worn it to school.

So far, being the Pizza Queen had been a lot of fun, even though I had not done any of the things Mr. Rush had talked about. At school on Friday the kids in my class had crowded around me.

"How does it feel to be the Pizza Queen?" Addie wanted to know.

"Is the crown heavy?" asked Pamela.

Natalie could not say anything. She just stared at me.

I smiled, and answered their questions in a queenly way.

Now it was TV commercial day. Guess what. Every single person in my big-house family was coming to the studio to watch me make my debut. Hannie and Nancy were coming, too.

A TV commercial is an Important Event, even for a queen.

Just before lunchtime, Nancy, Hannie, Sam, Kristy, and I piled into Charlie's Junk Bucket. (That is his car.) Everyone else piled into Daddy's van. Then we drove to the city of Stamford and found the TV studio.

The TV studio was just a regular building — low and flat and built of bricks. When we went inside we asked a man at a desk where we should go. He took one look at me and said, "Ah, the Pizza Queen." Then he pointed down a hallway. "First door on the right."

When we walked through that door we saw . . . equipment. We saw cameras and TVs and microphones on sticks. Emily began to cry. "Too scary!" she wailed. But then someone made the lights brighter. There. That was better. Kristy dried Emily's tears.

"Hello? Is Karen Brewer here?" called someone. A woman stepped between two big cameras. "Hi," she said. "I'm Marcy Jacobs."

And that was the beginning of my commercial debut.

First I sat behind a mirror with lights around it while a man named Gene put on my makeup and fixed my hair. Then I slipped into an outfit that the costume woman had chosen for me. (It was just a school outfit, a skirt and a shirt. At least I got to wear the crown.)

Then Marcy found me. "Are you ready to face the cameras?" she asked.

"Yes," I replied. "Will I have a lot of lines to memorize?"

"Just one," said Marcy. "Try saying, 'Mmm, this is the best pizza ever.' "

"Mmm, this is the best pizza ever," I repeated.

"Very good."

Guess how many times I had to say that line before Marcy and the director thought it was just right. Thirty-two. . . . Thirty-*two*. The other thing I was supposed to do was smile when a pair of hands placed the crown on my head. I was pretending I was being made the Pizza Queen again. Even though nobody had to say *any* lines, we had to do that sixteen times before the director liked it. Still, making a commercial was exciting. I smiled into the camera, and

Marcy brought me sodas, and every now and then someone would yell, "Makeup!" and then Gene would rush to me and touch up my rouge or brush my hair.

I could not wait to see myself on television.

Smile!

Sunday was as busy as Saturday had been. On Sunday, I went to a photography studio. Mr. Rush said he would need lots and lots of pictures of me — for a newspaper ad, for the billboard, and for posters to decorate Pizza Express, including a big one to go in the window.

Daddy drove me to the studio. Kristy and Hannie and Nancy came with us. Kristy just wanted to watch. Hannie and Nancy hoped the photographers might snap *their* pictures, too.

The photography studio was crowded and messy. Junk everywhere. I had never seen so much stuff. Clothes and furniture and toys and dishes and . . . stuff.

"We need these things in order to set up shots," explained Chris. (She was one of the photography assistants.) "Let's say we need a shot of you eating pizza at a kitchen table. Well, we could set that up easily, right here in the studio. We can set up almost anything."

"Cool," I said.

"Okay, Karen. Come with me to the makeup room."

More makeup. Goody!

Hannie and Nancy were allowed to come, too. They watched while a woman named Verna set my hair and put an awful lot of makeup on my face.

"Karen, you are very patient," Verna kept saying. "Can I get you anything? You need to sit here a few minutes longer. How about some juice? Or a soda? Don't worry about your lipstick. I can put it on again."

"Well," I said, "I would like some apple juice. So would my friends," I added.

Verna called to Marco who was another assistant. Here is the thing. Assistants were all over the place. There were Chris and Marco and a guy named Lenny. Someone named Ling was helping Verna. And then there were four photographers. The head photographer was Maureen. She was in charge.

When Nancy and Hannie and I finished our juice, and when Verna was happy with my hair and makeup, Chris led me back to the studio. She pointed to a corner which was set up to look like a booth at Pizza Express. Except for one thing. Pizza Express is sort of dark inside. The studio blazed with lights.

"Now you sit right here, Karen," said Chris.

I sat in the booth. Two bright lights were shining in my eyes. Two more shone down from overhead. Suddenly I was surrounded by people.

"How's the light?" asked Lenny.

"Her nose is already shiny," said Chris.

"Someone fix her dress. It's wrinkled," called Maureen.

Verna rushed forward. She smoothed my dress. Then she brushed some hair from my face and patted my nose with a powder puff.

Finally Maureen began taking pictures. When she stopped, Verna dashed over to me again and touched up my lipstick.

"Thirsty, Karen?" asked Marco.

"Tired yet?" asked Lenny.

"I'm a little thirsty again," I replied. "I think my friends and I need some refreshments. Is there any ginger ale?"

From across the room, Daddy frowned. But he did not say anything. Not until we were in the car on the way home. That was when I yawned and said, "I'm tired. Hannie, would you please sit in Nancy's lap so I could lie down for awhile?"

"No!" exclaimed both Hannie and Nancy. (I think they were mad because

Maureen had not taken their pictures.)

And Daddy said, "I know you worked hard today, Karen, and you must be awfully tired. But you are beginning to sound like a brat. That has got to stop."

"I'll say," muttered Hannie.

I pretended I had not heard her. I adjusted my crown. Then I looked out the window in a queenly way.

Free Pizza

By Wednesday I had been the Pizza Queen for six days. Maureen had sent some of my pictures over to Pizza Express, and Mr. Rush had put them up everywhere. Then he had asked Maureen to blow up one of the pictures. Maureen blew it up to the size of a poster. Mr. Rush hung it in the window. Every time I walked by Pizza Express, I saw my face.

A lot of other people saw it, too.

In school, I was famous. Kids I did not know at all — even big kids — stopped me in the hall or on the playground. They said things like, "Nice crown," or "Hey, it's the Pizza Queen!"

I was the most famous in my own classroom.

On Monday morning I was sitting at my desk reading. I was waiting for Hannie and Nancy to arrive.

"Hi, Karen!" someone called.

I looked up. It was just Pamela. Pamela Harding is my best enemy. I said hello but then I turned back to my book.

"Karen, do you want some stickers?" asked Pamela. She held out two sheets of animal stickers. "My big sister bought them for me yesterday. You can have some. Whichever ones you want."

I thought Pamela was kidding. She was being too nice. Pamela and I are never nice to each other unless Ms. Colman tells us to be.

"Oh . . . no, thanks," I replied.

"Go ahead," said Pamela. "Take some. I brought them in just for my friends. For my *friends,"* she repeated as Bobby Gianelli stopped to look at the stickers. (Bobby stuck his tongue out at Pamela, and she stuck hers out at him.)

I chose two puppy stickers.

One day at lunch I saw Natalie staring at me. "What's wrong?" I asked. Probably something was stuck to one of my front teeth. I would have to get it off. I could not go around wearing a beautiful crown on my head when I had lettuce stuck to my tooth.

Natalie shook her head. "Nothing," she answered. But she was still staring at me. Finally she said, "Karen? Do you feel like a different person when you wear the crown? Do you really feel like a queen?"

I thought for a moment. Then I replied, "Yes, I guess I do."

Natalie sighed. "I was hoping you would say that," she said. "Boy, I wish I could be a queen, even just for a day. Even just for a *minute.*"

* * *

On Wednesday morning, two first-graders poked their heads into Ms. Colman's room. They looked around until they saw me. I was sitting on the floor, playing jacks with Nancy and Hannie.

"There she is!" one of them whispered loudly.

"Where?"

"Over there. The one with the crown."

"Ooh, a beautiful, beautiful crown."

Not everyone liked the crown, though. Hank Reubens said it made my head look pointy. And Bobby Gianelli said, "Hey, Crownhead! Are you going to get free pizza for everyone? The Pizza Queen ought to be able to get free pizza. Can you do it?"

I thought about that. Mr. Rush had not said anything about free pizza. But he had been very nice. And very generous.

So I said, "Of course I can get free pizza." I was sure all I had to do was ask.

Big Karen

"Karen, what are you doing?" Andrew asked me one morning.

I was getting dressed for school. So I said, "I am getting dressed for school."

"I know," replied Andrew. "But what are *those*?" He pointed to my face.

"Oh. Sunglasses," I said.

"Why are you wearing them inside?"

"Because that is what famous people do."

"Why?"

"So no one will recognize them."

"But won't people recognize your crown?" asked Andrew.

Well, for heaven's sake. Little brothers are big pests.

I had been the Pizza Queen for a long time now. At least, it felt like a long time. The commercial was on TV. I had seen it four times. And my face was everywhere. Maureen and Mr. Rush sure had worked hard with those photos. They had even managed to put up the new billboard picture. The old Pizza King was gone. I, Karen Brewer the Pizza Queen, was there instead. A huge, *enormous*, GIGUNDO picture of me. I saw it every time we drove into or out of Stoneybrook. Everyone in my two families had seen it, too. Emily had started calling me Big Karen.

That morning Seth drove Nancy and me to school. I was wearing my crown and the sunglasses. "Be sure to take the sunglasses off when you go inside," said Seth as he pulled up in front of the school. "Put on your pink glasses."

"Okay," I replied. But behind my back my fingers were crossed. Seth did not understand about famous people.

Nancy and I walked through the hallway to our classroom.

"Excuse me, are you the Pizza Queen?" I heard someone say.

I turned around. A boy was following Nancy and me. I think he was a third-grader. He was holding a pad of paper and a pencil.

"Yes," I answered.

"Could I have your autograph?" he asked.

I just love giving out autographs. A lot of kids had asked for them. But I knew that movie stars always pretend they are *very* busy. So I said, "I don't know. The bell is going to ring soon."

"*Please?* It will only take a second. The paper is right here." The boy held the pad in front of my face.

"Well, okay," I said. I scribbled *Karen Brewer, Pizza Queen* on the paper.

"Thanks! Thanks a lot!" cried the boy. Then he ran off.

I turned to Nancy and sighed. "My, but being a movie star is tiring."

When we reached our classroom, Hannie was already there. I marched over to her and said, "Guess why we are late. Someone wanted my autograph. Again." I paused. Then I added, "My, but being a movie star is tiring."

Nancy and Hannie glanced at each other. "Karen, you are not a movie star," said Nancy. "You have not made a movie."

"You are hardly even a TV star," added Hannie.

"She is just a billboard star," called Hank from across the room.

"Hey, Karen, when are we going to get our free pizza?" asked Bobby.

"Oh, any day now," I told him. "I promise."

To tell the truth, I had not remembered to ask Mr. Rush about the pizza, but I did not think it would be a problem.

"You promise? Really?" said Pamela. She looked as if she did not believe me. When I thought about it, Pamela was not so nice to me anymore. No more stickers or friendly talks.

Even so, I said, "*Yes*. I promise." I would talk to Mr. Rush as soon as I had time. But being the Pizza Queen kept me awfully busy.

Hootie's New Home

*B*rrrrrrring!

The last bell of the day rang. And the door to my classroom opened. Guess who stepped inside. Andrew and Mommy. It was Friday afternoon and we were going to bring Hootie home with us. Starting on Monday, the workmen would be fixing up our classroom.

"Boys and girls," said Ms. Colman, "remember what to do on Monday morning. Go to the cafeteria. Do not come here to our classroom."

My friends and I ran to our cubbies. We put on our sweaters and jackets. The other kids began to leave, and I ran to Mommy.

"These are Hootie's things," Ms. Colman was saying to Mommy. "Here are his dishes and toys and food."

"And I know all about taking care of Hootie," I told Mommy.

Andrew and I carried the bag out of the classroom. Mommy and Ms. Colman carried Hootie in his cage. They loaded the cage into our car. When we reached the little house, Mommy put Hootie in my room. Andrew and I tried to make Hootie feel at home.

"Here is your food," I said to Hootie.

"And here are your toys," added Andrew.

We watched Hootie. He sniffed around. He tasted his food. Then I said, "Andrew, I think I would like some time alone with Hootie." So Andrew left the room.

I took off my crown and sunglasses. I put on my pink glasses. Then I lifted Hootie

out of the cage and lay on the floor with him. "This is your new home," I said. "Your home for a week. I think you will be happy here. Guess what. You have two roommates. I am one, and the other is Emily Junior. Her cage is right over there, across the room." I carried Hootie to Emily's cage. I let him peek at her through the glass. I did not know if they would want to play together, though. I decided that might not be a good idea.

"Karen! Telephone!" Mommy called.

I put Hootie in his cage and ran for the phone. "Hello?" I said.

"Hi, Karen. It's me, Pamela."

"Hi," I replied. (Now why was Pamela calling?)

"Um, Karen, I am going to Pizza Express tomorrow with my sister, and I was wondering if I could ask for that free pizza."

"Well . . ." I said slowly. "I — I guess you better not. Not yet."

"Okay." Pamela sounded disappointed.

I had just hung up the phone when it

rang again. This time Bobby Gianelli was calling. And I had a feeling I knew why.

"Karen," he said, "I forgot to ask you about something today. I forgot to ask you about free pizza. When are we going to get it? You will not be the Pizza Queen forever."

Hmm. That was true. In a couple of weeks I would have to give my crown back. Somebody else would be the Pizza Queen or the Pizza King.

"You will get the pizza soon," I said to Bobby. "I promise."

"But you promised before."

"This time I *really* promise."

As soon as I was off the phone, I went looking for Mommy. "Do you think I can get free pizza for my friends?" I asked her. "Since I am the Pizza Queen."

Mommy shook her head. "Sorry, honey. I don't think so. Mr. Rush did not mention it. Besides, he is paying you a lot of money. And no," Mommy went on, "you may not ask Mr. Rush about it."

I couldn't? Uh-oh.

Happy Birthday, Dear Joey

On Saturday morning I had a talk with Hootie. "All right, I am not going to be around much this weekend," I told him. "I will be very busy. I am sorry to have to leave you, but you will not be alone. Emily Junior is right over there in her cage. See? She can keep you company. And maybe Andrew will visit you." I paused. "Rocky might visit you, too. He is a cat. But don't worry. He cannot get in your cage. At least I don't think he can. So just relax. I am leaving now, but I will be back later."

I really did have an awfully busy weekend. I had to make two appearances as the Pizza Queen. Today I was going to Bellair's Department Store. Tomorrow, Sunday, I was going to appear at a birthday party at Pizza Express.

Seth drove me to Bellair's. The people at the store were raising money to help homeless people. They wanted me to wear my crown (but not my sunglasses), hold out a box, and call, "Every penny helps! Please give!"

"Seth, what are homeless people?" I asked on the way to the store.

"Not 'what,' honey, 'who.' *Who* are homeless people."

"Okay, *who* are they?"

"They are people who do not have any homes."

"Then where do they live?"

"In shelters. Or sometimes in parks or on the street."

"What do they eat?"

"Whatever they can find. Sometimes

people give them money for food."

"Are children ever homeless?" I wanted to know.

"Sometimes," Seth replied.

I hoped I could raise a lot of money that day. I asked every person I saw to drop some money in my box.

My job on Sunday was easier. A boy named Joey McGrath was turning five years old. He had asked to hold his birthday party at Pizza Express. He and his guests were going to eat pizza and cake and ice cream. They were going to watch a magic show by Pockets the Clown. And they were going to meet me, the Pizza Queen.

The good thing about Joey's party was that I got to eat pizza and cake and ice cream, too. Also I got to watch Pockets put on his magic show. Guess what Pockets could do. He could break an egg into a hat, pour in some milk, tap the hat with his wand — and make a dove fly out. If I put an egg and milk into *my* hat, I would just make a mess. And some adult would probably be mad at me. Pockets could also pull scarves out of his mouth. And he cut a rope in half, and then the rope put itself back together again. Pockets was a true magician.

The bad thing about Joey's birthday party was that I did not know the kids. When Joey's father brought his cake to him, I sang, "Happy birthday, dear Joey," with everyone else. But I felt funny, since I had not met Joey before. Then Mr. Rush handed me a big present and he said, "Go give Joey this gift, Karen. Tell him it is from the Pizza Queen."

But it was not *really* from me, and Joey knew that.

I was glad when the party was over.

"Mommy, what time is it?" I asked on the way home.

"Almost five o'clock, sweetie," she replied.

Five o'clock. Boo and bullfrogs. The weekend was almost over and I had not had time to play with Nancy or Hannie. I had not even called them. I played with Emily Junior that night instead. And Hootie. And Andrew. But I missed my friends. I was not sure I liked being *so* busy.

Before I went to sleep I kissed Hootie good night. "I hope you are enjoying your new home," I said. Then I lay in bed and thought about going to school in the cafeteria the next day.

Karen the Pest

*B*ang, *bang, bang. Clunk, clunk, clunk.*

I peered into my classroom. It was full of workmen. They were standing on ladders and bending over toolboxes. One was lying on his back with his head under the radiator. They were hammering and banging and talking. Also they were drinking coffee. The room smelled of coffee and paint. I saw brushes and cans lined up.

"Hey, Karen! Did you forget?" called someone. Natalie Springer was hurrying through the hallway. "It's Monday. We go to the cafeteria, remember? The workmen are in our room today."

"I know. I just wanted to see what they are doing," I replied.

Natalie and I walked to the cafeteria. Natalie gazed at my crown. "How long do you get to wear that?" she asked.

"For another week or so," I told her.

"How about the sunglasses?"

"Forever. I think I will just keep wearing them. Except when I need to wear my other glasses. It is good practice for when I really am a great big movie star."

Natalie and I walked into the cafeteria. Our classmates were running everywhere. Bobby was pretending to serve drinks from the soda machine. Pamela was giving Jannie and Leslie a ride on a food cart.

"Uh-oh," I said. "We are going to get in tr — "

"Ahem."

I whirled around. Ms. Colman was standing behind Natalie and me. She did not look a bit happy.

In a flash, everyone was sitting at two of the long cafeteria tables.

We folded our hands in front of us.

That morning Ms. Colman gave us a big talk about our behavior. Then we got to work. We worked on reading and spelling and math. Guess what. There was no blackboard in the cafeteria, so we could sit wherever we wanted. I sat between Hannie and Nancy.

After a few hours, the first-graders came into the cafeteria. It was their lunchtime. So we had to leave. We worked in one of their classrooms for awhile. Then it was *our* lunchtime, and then recess. After recess we moved into the auditorium.

Ms. Colman told us to open our science books. She talked to us about the sun and the planets. But we were having trouble paying attention. Ricky was busy prying old gum off the bottom of his seat. The twins were trying to peek behind the curtains at the windows. Addie kept moving her wheelchair up and down the aisle.

Finally Ms. Colman sighed. "All right," she said. "I think you need a break."

"Yes!" I cried. I leaped to my feet. So did everyone else. Bobby, Ricky, and Hank began a game of Kleenex tag. Hannie and Nancy and I raced up the steps to the stage.

"Let's put on a show!" exclaimed Nancy.

"Okay!" I cried. "I know what to do." I settled my crown on my head. "I will now perform my television commercial," I announced.

I performed it five times. I would have kept on going, but Pamela said, "Tsk. You are a pest, Karen." Everyone nodded their heads. Even Nancy and Hannie. Even *Natalie*.

And Bobby stopped his game of Kleenex tag to say, "You know, the contest is on at Pizza Express to choose the next king or queen."

I closed my eyes. I did not want to think about that.

Lonely

On Tuesday my friends and I went to the cafeteria again. But this time, when the first-graders came in, Ms. Colman did not move us to their classroom. Instead she said, "Boys and girls, the weather is beautiful today. So we will try working outside until lunchtime."

Oh, boy. I just love working outside. When Ms. Colman takes us to the playground, we always sit under the same tree. Sometimes she reads to us, sometimes we write stories or poems, sometimes we work in our workbooks. On that Tuesday, Ms. Colman read to us from a very funny book called *The Mouse and the Motorcycle*, by Beverly Cleary. But after a while she noticed that Nancy was looking for four-leaf clovers, and I was braiding Hannie's hair, and Ricky was rubbing two sticks together trying to start a campfire. Then a kindergarten class ran outside for recess and we all turned to watch them.

"Okay," said Ms. Colman, "I think you need another break." She closed the book. "Fifteen minutes," she added.

Nancy and Hannie and I headed for a hopscotch court, but I heard a small voice say, " 'Scuze me. Are you the Pizza Queen?"

A bunch of kindergarteners were following my friends and me.

"Yes, I am," I replied.

"I like your crown," said one.

"Do you remember me?" asked another. "I was at Joey McGrath's birthday party. And so were you, Pizza Queen."

"I was there, too," said another little kid.

"Pizza Queen, could I have your autograph?"

"Could I try on your crown?"

"Sure, sure," I replied. I wrote my name on a couple of pieces of paper from my notebook. Then I let two of the kids try on my crown. (I watched them *very* carefully.)

"Thanks! Thank you!" cried the kids.

"Would you like me to perform my TV commercial?" I asked.

Of course they wanted me to. I put it on four times. Then I turned around to see if Nancy and Hannie and my other friends were watching. But they were not. They were playing hopscotch and catch and jump rope and kickball. Do you know what? I felt an intsy bit lonely.

Oops

Since I had felt lonely that day in school, I played with Nancy all afternoon. We pretended we were Lovely Ladies having a tea party. Then Mrs. Dawes let us take Nancy's baby brother for a walk. After that we ran around my yard for a while. By dinnertime I felt much better, not lonely at all. I ate a big supper.

Then I went to my room. This is the homework Ms. Colman had given us at the end of the day: Think about ways you can help the environment. I sat on my bed.

Hmm. What kinds of things could *kids* do? What could *I* do?

While I thought, I gazed around my room. I looked at my desk. I looked at Emily in her cage. I looked at Hootie's cage. I saw the cage, but not Hootie. I jumped up. I ran to the cage.

Where was Hootie?

"Hootie? Are you there?" I cried. "Where are you hiding?" The top of Hootie's cage was half off. It looked as if it had been moved to the side. How had that happened? Had Hootie figured out how to escape? (He might have. He is a very smart guinea pig.) Had Rocky gone after Hootie? (He might have. He is a cat.)

"Hootie! Hootie!" I called. I rummaged around in his cage. Maybe Hootie was hiding in the shavings.

But Hootie was gone.

"Oh, Emily," I said to my rat. "I wish you could talk. Then you could tell me what happened to Hootie."

Emily just peered at me from her nest of

newspapers and shavings. I ran to my door. I was about to yell for Mommy. Then I remembered something. I remembered the promises I had made when I had asked if I could take care of Hootie. I had promised Mommy that Hootie would be no trouble. I had promised to be responsible. Well, now there was big trouble. And I certainly did not seem very responsible.

I could not tell anybody that Hootie was missing. I would have to solve this problem all by myself.

I decided to search my room. (I closed my door so no one would see what I was doing.) "Hootie! Hootie!" I called softly. "Hootie, come out. Please come back home. I miss you."

I looked under my bed and under my desk and under my chair and under everything. I got a flashlight and shined it behind the bureau. Then I shined it around inside my closet. I looked in every shoe, and under all the junk. I even looked on the shelf above my clothes.

No Hootie.

I carried the flashlight into the hall. I looked up and down the hall. I looked in Andrew's bedroom and in Seth and Mommy's bedroom. I looked in the bathrooms.

No Hootie.

At bedtime, Hootie was still missing. I made an announcement.

"Mommy, Seth, Andrew," I said, "I am very sorry, but I think Rocky has been going after Hootie." (That was not a lie.) "So I have decided to keep the door to my room closed. That way, Hootie will be safe." (That *was* sort of a lie.) "Please do not go in my room."

If nobody went in my room, nobody would notice that Hootie was not in his cage. To help my family remember to stay out, I made a sign. It said, *Privit. Do Not Enter*. I hung it on my door.

Finally I went to bed. But I did not sleep very well. I kept waking up and calling softly, "Hootie! Hootie!" But in the morning, Hootie was still missing.

Worries

It was Wednesday. I had woken up early because I had not slept well. Even though I knew it was a silly thing to do, I checked Hootie's cage. I did not think he would be in it, but I checked anyway. Then, while the rest of my little-house family slept, I looked around my room again. I looked under things, behind things, and in the closet.

No Hootie.

By the time Seth drove me to school that day I was keeping a terrible secret: Hootie was still missing. I did not think anyone in my family would find out, though. The door to my room was closed, and my sign was hanging up. And I did not plan to *tell* anyone about Hootie.

That morning I tried to concentrate. I tried to pay attention to Ms. Colman. This was not easy. I was worried about Hootie. Plus, we were working in the cafeteria again. I could smell chicken roasting. I watched a deliveryman bring in a load of ice-cream bars. I listened to the cooks talking.

And then into the cafeteria walked Mr. Rush, a photographer, and a woman holding a pad of paper. Mr. Rush waved to me. Then he talked to Ms. Colman for a few minutes.

"Class," said Ms. Colman when they were finished talking, "I would like you to meet Mr. Rush. He is the owner of Pizza Express. He phoned me yesterday and said he might drop by school this morning. He has brought along some people from the newspaper. They are working on an article about the Pizza Express contest. They would like to take some pictures of Karen during her last days as the Pizza Queen."

I sat up straight in my seat. I smiled. I adjusted my crown. "Where do you want me to pose?" I asked Mr. Rush.

"Oh, just stay where you are," he replied. "We want pictures of you and your friends working at school, just like on any day."

"You want pictures of *us*?" said Bobby.

"Really?" squeaked Natalie.

"How does my hair look?" whispered Pamela.

The photographer walked around the room. He snapped pictures everywhere. I was not even in some of them. The woman walked around the room, too. She asked us questions and wrote down what we said. She asked me if I had enjoyed my reign as Pizza Queen. She asked my friends how they had felt about going to school with the Pizza Queen.

"It was wonderful," said Natalie. "I like knowing a famous person."

But Pamela said, "Karen is a pain in the neck."

And Bobby said, "The Pizza Queen does not keep her promises."

I stuck my tongue out at Pamela and Bobby.

Then the photographer said, "How about a group shot? Everybody together. Ms. Colman, too. Over here at this table."

The photographer took five pictures. Then my friends began talking and laughing. Audrey chased Hank around a table. Addie gave Tammy a ride on the back of her wheelchair. And . . . guess what. Bobby Gianelli walked right over to Mr. Rush and said, "When are we going to get the free pizza?"

"Excuse me?" said Mr. Rush.

"Karen said she would get free pizza for us, because she is the Pizza Queen. Only she has not done it."

"And soon she will not be the Pizza

Queen anymore," added Hank.

A bunch of kids had crowded around Mr. Rush. They were all asking for their free pizza. Mr. Rush looked confused. I heard him say, "We'll see, we'll see." Then Ms. Colman rescued him.

I was *so* embarrassed. I wished I could just crawl somewhere and hide. Soon everyone would know I had lied about the pizza. And soon everyone would know I had lost Hootie.

I was in a gigundo mess.

16

Hide-and-Seek

I could not wait to go home after school. I did not want to hear any more questions about pizza. I did not want to hear about being a pain in the neck or about not keeping my promises.

I did want to look for Hootie, though.

I ran up the stairs and down the hall to my room. I opened the door. I closed it behind me. Then I peered into Hootie's cage. Of course, he was not in it. How could he have gotten into my room when the door was closed? And even if he had returned, would he have jumped back into his cage by himself? Probably not.

I decided to search the house again. I would search one room at a time. And I would look in every place I could think of.

I looked in Andrew's room first. Maybe Andrew had wanted to play with Hootie so he had taken Hootie from the cage and hidden him in his room. But I did not find Hootie there, even though I looked *very* hard. I did find one of my sneakers, though. I tossed it into my room.

Next I searched the bathrooms. That did not take too long. After that I searched Mommy and Seth's room. Then I went downstairs.

I was on my hands and knees peering behind a couch when I heard Mommy say, "Karen? What are you doing?"

Uh-oh. I could not tell Mommy what I was *really* doing.

"I — I am, um, playing hide-and-seek with Rocky," I said. I stood up. "Oh, Rocky!" I called. "Where are you? You have

found a very good hiding place this time."
I ran into the playroom.

Andrew was there. "Are you really playing hide-and-seek with Rocky?" he wanted to know. "Can I play, too?"

"Well — " I started to say. And just then Rocky wandered into the room.

"Hey! There's Rocky!" cried Andrew. "He is not hiding at all."

"I guess he got tired of playing," I said. "Oh well."

I went back to searching for Hootie. While I was looking for him I found my missing troll, a quarter, a poem I had written, and the other sneaker. But I did not find Hootie.

I sat down on the floor in the dining room. What if I did not find Hootie in the next five days? Also, what would my friends do when they learned the truth about the pizza? They would think I was a lot worse than just a pain in the neck.

I gulped. I was about to burst into tears when the phone rang.

Good News

"Karen!" called Mommy. "Phone for you. It's Mr. Rush."

Mr. Rush? Oops. I was sure he wanted to know why my friends had been bugging him about free pizza. Or maybe he was calling to tell me it was time to turn in my crown.

I took the phone from Mommy. "Hello?" I said.

"Hi, Karen. It's Mr. Rush from Pizza Express. I enjoyed meeting your classmates this morning. They are very . . . energetic."

"I — I know. Um, Mr. Rush, about the free pizza," I began. (From across the kitchen Mommy sent me a FROWN.)

"That is just why I am calling, Karen," said Mr. Rush. "I heard your friends asking about the free pizza, and I was wondering something. I was wondering if you would like to invite your class to a party at Pizza Express. I will serve free pizza and sodas to everyone. It will be my way of saying thank you for doing such a wonderful job as the Pizza Queen. We could have the party after school on Friday. How does that sound?"

"Oh! Oh, Mr. Rush, it sounds great! Thank you so much! I will have to talk to my friends, but I am sure they will think it is great, too. Here comes my mom. She wants to talk to you now."

Even though I had not found Hootie, I began to feel better. I looked cheerfully for Hootie until dinnertime. After supper I did my homework. Then I looked for Hootie

81

again. The next morning I put on my crown and my sunglasses. When I reached the cafeteria I said to my classmates, "Guess what. Wonderful news. You know the free pizza I promised you?"

Everyone crowded around me. "Yes?" they said.

"Well, I can give you something better than just pizza. I can give you an actual pizza party. It will be at Pizza Express tomorrow after school. You will get pizza *and* soda. And all because I am the Pizza Queen. I *told* you I could get you pizza, and now I got you a whole party."

All day long, whenever I could, I reminded my friends about the wonderful pizza party I would be giving them the next day.

But guess what. When I was in the bathroom I heard Pamela say to Audrey, "Karen thinks she is so great. She brags all the time."

"Yeah, just because she is the stupid Pizza Queen," said Audrey.

Later, on the playground, Hannie and Nancy and I asked Audrey if she wanted to play hopscotch with us. Audrey shook her head. "No, thank you," she replied. "Karen is too obnoxious." Then she repeated her big word. "Ob-nox-ious." She flounced away.

"What does obnoxious mean?" I asked Nancy.

"I think it means you are a pest."

At the end of the day Hannie rushed over to me. "Guess what I just heard," she said. "Pamela does not want to come to the pizza party. Audrey and the twins might not come either."

"But I thought everyone wanted free pizza so badly!" I cried.

"They did," said Bobby as he walked by us. "But they do not want to eat it with Miss *Obnoxious* Pizza Queen."

"Am I really obnoxious?" I asked Hannie.

"Well . . ." She paused. "Maybe you could take off the sunglasses. That might help."

I took them off. I took off the crown, too. I thought about the way I had invited my friends to the pizza party. Maybe I *had* been showing off an intsy bit. Maybe I *had* been a little obnoxious.

It was Thursday afternoon. The party was supposed to take place in one day. I could not tell Mr. Rush that nobody wanted to come to the party. I had to decide what to do about it.

18

Karen's Pizza Party

When I woke up on Friday morning, I rolled over in bed. I looked at my dresser. The night before, I had left my crown and sunglasses on the dresser. That was where I had left them every night before I went to sleep. Then I could put them on the moment I woke up. This morning I did not put them on, though. And I did not bring them to school.

"Hey, Pizza Queen!" Bobby yelled when he saw me. "Where is your crown? Aren't you the queen anymore?"

"I am still the queen," I replied. "But I do not think I need to wear the crown all the time. Or the sunglasses."

"How come?" asked Bobby.

"You'll see."

This is what I had decided to do about the pizza party: Stop being obnoxious. If I was not obnoxious, maybe my friends would come to the party. It was worth a try. I talked to Ms. Colman.

"Ms. Colman," I said. "May I say something to our class after you make the announcements? It is very important."

"All right," replied my teacher.

That morning I stood next to Ms. Colman in the cafeteria. I looked around at my classmates. I said, "I know I have been obnoxious. I have listened to the things you said. And I am sorry. I made promises I could not keep, and I bragged a lot — "

"And you showed off," added Pamela.

"And I showed off," I agreed. "Anyway, I am almost finished being the Pizza Queen. And I am really finished being obnoxious.

So will you please come to the party? Mr. Rush still says we can have it. It will be at Pizza Express after school today."

Mommy drove Nancy and Andrew and me to Pizza Express that afternoon.

"Do you think anyone will come to the party?" I whispered to Nancy.

"I hope so," she replied.

Guess what. Everyone came. Ms. Colman, too.

I began to smile. I could not *stop* smiling.

"Thank you for coming," said Mr. Rush when my friends and I were sitting down. "Help yourselves to pizza and sodas. And have fun!"

I have never seen so much pizza in my whole life.

Neither had Andrew. "This is even better than Chuckie's Happy House," he said.

"Much better," I agreed.

I sat at a table with Nancy and Hannie and Andrew. I was still not wearing my crown. I tried not to be obnoxious. I did not perform my TV commercial. I did not offer people my autograph. I just sat in my spot and ate pizza and drank soda and laughed.

I think my friends had a good time. Bobby and Ricky made up imaginary pizzas. Their best one was peanut butter pizza with whipped cream, raisins, and sardines, hold the olives.

Addie and Audrey and the twins held a joke-telling contest. They decided the winning joke was: What time is it when an elephant sits on the fence? Time to get a new fence! (I have heard that joke one million times before, but I still think it is funny.)

I *know* Pamela had fun at the party. That is because when it was over, she said to me, "Thank you, Karen. The party was great."

Everyone else thanked me, too. And of course we thanked Mr. Rush. Now if only I could find Hootie. I was supposed to bring him back to school on Monday. In just three days.

Behind the Refrigerator

When Andrew and I returned to our house, we had to pack our knapsacks. Soon Mommy would drive us to Daddy's. It was the beginning of a big-house weekend.

I packed in my room with the door closed. While I packed, I worried. And I talked to Emily Junior. "I bet you know where Hootie is, don't you?" I said to my rat. "I wish you would tell him to come back. I cannot even look for him this weekend. And on Monday — "

Knock, knock. Someone was at my door.

"Who is it?" I called.

"It's Mommy," said Mommy. And then she walked right into my room.

She was holding Hootie.

I let out a shriek. "Hootie!" I cried. "Where have you been?"

"I found him behind the refrigerator," replied Mommy. "Karen, how long has he been missing?" (Mommy was frowning again.)

"Um, since Tuesday," I admitted.

"Since *Tuesday*! Karen, why didn't you say anything?"

"Well . . . well . . . I don't know. I kept looking for Hootie. I just hoped I would find him. I promised you Hootie would not be a problem. So I tried to take care of this myself."

"Oh, Karen," said Mommy. "I appreciate that. But you cannot let a guinea pig run loose in the house. Anything could happen to him. And if Hootie had gotten outdoors I do not think we would have seen him

again. As it is, he probably has not eaten in three days."

I peered at Hootie. "I don't know. He looks pretty fat to me."

Mommy held him out and looked at him, too. "Actually, he does," she said, smiling. "I wonder what he's been eating."

"I bet we will find a big hole in a box of crackers or cereal," I said.

Mommy set Hootie in his cage. Then she sat on my bed. "Karen, do you realize that Hootie is very lucky? You are both lucky that Rocky did not go after Hootie, that Hootie did not get trapped somewhere, that he did not go near an electrical socket, and that he did not escape outside. Not telling me about your problem," said Mommy, "was not the best thing to do. It was not safe for Hootie. Do you understand?"

"Yes," I replied.

"I know you were trying to be responsible. But the most responsible thing to have done, when you realized Hootie was missing, was tell a grown-up. I hope you will remember that. Making choices can be hard, but always try to make the safest choice if anyone or anything is in danger. Will you promise me that?"

"Yes," I said again.

"Now," said Mommy, "as fat as Hootie is, I bet he is hungry."

"He probably has not eaten any lettuce or carrots," I agreed.

"Why don't you fix a special meal for Hootie?" suggested Mommy.

So I did. All his favorite things.

While he was eating, Mommy looked at the latch on Hootie's cage. "It is very loose," she said. "Anyone could have knocked the lid off, even Rocky. Then Hootie could have escaped easily."

Mommy and I fixed the latch on the top of Hootie's cage. We made sure it was fastened *very* tightly. Then it was time to go to Daddy's.

So Hootie came with me to the big house. And on Monday he went back to school, back to our new, clean, beautiful classroom.

20

The New Pizza Queen

It was almost my last day as Pizza Queen. At Pizza Express, people had been filling out lots and lots of those entry forms. An enormous barrel was full of them. Soon Mr. Rush would choose one, and then he would say, "And the winner is . . ."

On Thursday, Mommy picked me up after school. She brought Andrew and my crown with her. I had not been wearing the crown much anymore.

Mommy drove us to Pizza Express. On the way, we passed a couple of posters with my picture on it. And Andrew said, "I saw you on TV this morning, Karen."

Soon no one would see me on TV. The posters would be taken down. And someone else's face would be plastered on the billboard. No more Big Karen. In just a little while, Mr. Rush would draw a name out of the barrel, and then I would give my crown to the new Pizza Queen or King.

"Good afternoon, Karen," said Mr. Rush when we arrived. "Come on and take your place."

Mr. Rush led me inside Pizza Express and helped me into the window. A throne had been set there. It was the one I had seen Rodney Harris, the old Pizza King, sitting on, on the last day of his reign. Now it was my turn.

I settled myself on the throne. I adjusted my crown. Then I looked at the crowd outside. I saw Mommy and Andrew and Nancy and Hannie and Linny and Ricky and Addie and Bobby and Natalie and Pamela and the rest of the kids in my class. I saw newspaper reporters and people with cameras. I saw old people and young people and tall people and short people. Almost everyone was waving at me, so I waved back in a queenly way.

From outside I could hear Mr. Rush say, "Good afternoon!" (The people in the crowd stopped talking.) "Thank you for coming," he went on. "Welcome to the Pizza Express Royalty Contest. Today we will choose another new Pizza Queen or King. And we will say good-bye to Karen Brewer, the reigning queen. Now without further ado . . ."

Mr. Rush reached into that barrel. He shuffled around all those entry forms. Finally he chose one. He drew it out.

"And the winner is," he said, "Natalie Springer."

Natalie *Springer*? I could not have heard right. Mr. Rush must have said some other name, like Natalia Spangler or something. But no, out in the audience the kids in my class were screaming and cheering and jumping up and down. Then they moved aside, and Natalie and her father made their way to Mr. Rush.

My mouth had dropped open. The new Pizza Queen was another kid from Ms. Colman's room? The new Pizza Queen was dowdy Natalie with the droopy socks? Then I remembered Natalie gazing at my crown, and Natalie asking if I really felt like a queen. I began to smile.

A few minutes later, Mr. Rush and Natalie were standing next to me in the window. Mr. Rush lifted the crown, the lovely crown, from my head. He set it on Natalie's head. Then Natalie sat on the throne. She looked so nervous I thought she was going to cry. So I leaned over and said, "Natalie, see all those people out there? They are waving and smiling — at *you*. So wave and smile back."

Natalie waved a little. Then a smile crept over her face.

"Natalie, I have to tell you a few things," I whispered. "They are very important. Do

not wear the crown *all* the time, okay? And do not make promises you cannot keep. And most of all, try not to be obnoxious. But have fun."

"Okay," replied Natalie.

Then Mr. Rush and I left her in the window.

About the Author

ANN M. MARTIN lives in New York City and loves animals, especially cats. She has two cats of her own, Mouse and Rosie.

Other books by Ann M. Martin that you might enjoy are *Stage Fright*; *Me and Katie (the Pest)*; and the books in *The Baby-sitters Club* series.

Ann likes ice cream and *I Love Lucy*. And she has her own little sister, whose name is Jane.